MORNING IN AMERICA

ONI PRESS

AN ONI PRESS PRODUCTION

WRITTEN BY MAGDALENE VISAGGIO
ILLUSTRATED BY CLAUDIA AGUIRRE
LETTERED BY ZAKK SAAM

Designed by Dylan Todd and Sonja Synak
Edited by Ari Yarwood

Published by Oni Press, Inc.

Joe Nozemack, founder & chief financial officer
James Lucas Jones, publisher
Sarah Gaydos, editor in chief
Charlie Chu, v.p. of creative & business development
Brad Rooks, director of operations
Margot Wood, director of sales
Amber O'Neill, special projects manager
Troy Look, director of design & production
Kate Z. Stone, senior graphic designer
Sonja Synak, graphic designer
Angie Knowles, digital prepress lead
Robin Herrera, senior editor
Ari Yarwood, senior editor
Michelle Nguyen, executive assistant
Jung Lee, logistics coordinator

1319 SE Martin Luther King, Jr. Blvd.
Suite 240
Portland, OR 97214

onipress.com
facebook.com/onipress
twitter.com/onipress
onipress.tumblr.com
instagram.com/onipress

@MagsVisaggs
@claudiaguirre
@ZakkSaam

First Edition: October 2019

ISBN: 978-1-62010-657-0
eISBN: 978-1-62010-658-7

1 2 3 4 5 6 7 8 9 10

Library of Congress Control Number: 2019936545

Printed in China.

CHAPTER 1

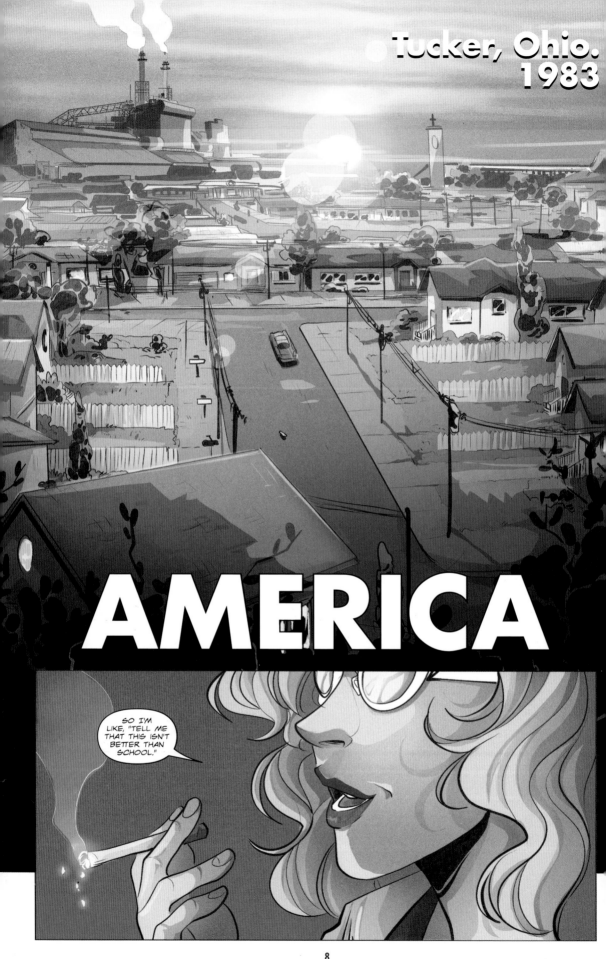

THE SICK SISTERS

ONE WEEK BEFORE THE END OF THE WORLD.

MORNING.

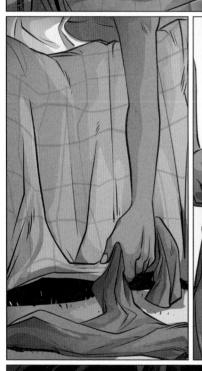

I KEEP TELLING YOU, I'M **LOOKING.** THERE JUST AREN'T ANY UNION JOBS IN TUCKER ANYMORE.

WE'RE RUNNING OUT OUR **SAVINGS,** LUIS. WE'RE RUNNING OUT **FAST.**

THAT'S WHY, FOR THE FORESEEABLE FUTURE, WE'LL BE PARTNERING WITH THE KNOX COUNTY POLICE DEPARTMENT TO ENSURE STUDENT SAFETY.

TO INTRODUCE THE NEW SECURITY MEASURES....

NANCY! SIT HERE!

I'M COMING, GEEZ.

HEY, RONNIE.

NANCE.

OHMYGOD I WAS JUST TELLING VERONICA ABOUT THIS BOOK I'M READING WITH DISAPPEARANCES JUST LIKE THE ONES WE'VE HAD LATELY, EXCEPT IT WAS ALIENS AND EVERYONE WAS COVERING IT UP.

ASH, I DON'T THINK--

IT WAS THIS BIG CONSPIRACY BEING MASTERMINDED BY ALIENS SO THEY COULD SLOWLY TAKE OVER THE ENTIRE PLANET.

ALRIGHT. COAST IS--

EVEN BETTER.

WHAT'D I MISS?

'NOTHER MISSING KID.

HOW *ENTIRELY* DULL.

I DUNNO. NETA, TWO IN A WEEK IS A LOT. THEY'RE PUTTING IN ALL THIS NEW SECURITY.

SECURITY-SHMECURITY. ANYONE TRIES TO TOUCH ME, I JUST TAKE THEIR BALLS.

WHAT IF IT'S A GIRL?

OVARY-ECTOMY.

TWO IN A WEEK, *FOURTH* DISAPPEARANCE OVERALL...

THIS WHOLE THING IS STARTING TO FEEL REALLY WEIRD.

AND WHAT IF IT'S **ALIENS**.

ALIENS.

ALIENS.

WHY WOULD IT BE ALIENS?

IT'S ALL HERE IN **MORTAL DIVIDE**, ELLEN!

ALIENS WANT TO **DESTROY HUMANITY**, SO THEY SPEND YEARS LAYING ALL THIS, YOU KNOW, **GROUNDWORK** AND STUFF? THEY START SMALL AND GO FROM THERE.

TAKING OVER A SMALL TOWN LIKE TUCKER IS **ONLY THE BEGINNING**.

THAT **NEW FACTORY**, YOU KNOW? IT'S THE PERFECT COVER. IT JUST OPENED BUT **NOBODY SEEMS TO WORK THERE?** OR EVEN **KNOWS**--

PSSSH. LITERALLY EVERYONE WOULD HAVE TO BE IN ON IT.

AND BESIDES, THE **MONEY** THAT FACTORY IS PUMPING INTO THE TOWN IS THE ONLY THING KEEPING TUCKER ALIVE.

EVERYONE KNOWS THAT.

The treaty that ended the Mexican War was called: _____

A. The Treaty of Guadalupe Hidalgo
B. The Treaty of Veracruz
C. The Peace of Texas
The Honda Accord

HEY, DOLLFACE. HOW'D IT GO?

CRITICAL FAILURE.

YEAAAH, I DIDN'T DO A LOT BETTER. I'M THINKING D, D-MINUS TERRITORY.

HISTORY IS *STUPID.*

GOD! I KNOW, RIGHT?

THE MEXICAN WAR WAS DUMB AND AWFUL AND I DON'T CARE WHAT THE TREATY WAS CALLED!

GUADALUPE HIDALGO.

THAT'S THE SHIT I'M TALKING ABOUT! WHY DOES THAT MATTER? NOBODY'S GONNA QUIZ ME ON THIS WITH A GUN TO MY HEAD. MEANWHILE NOBODY IS TESTING ME ABOUT *SIOUXSIE AND THE BANSHEES.*

WHY ISN'T *THAT* IMPORTANT?

THAT'S WHAT MAKES US FAILURES IN THEIR *SYSTEM,* DUDE. BECAUSE WE'D RATHER LIVE THAN WORK.

BECAUSE WE'RE THE *REAL* ONES. YOU AND ME.

HEH.

YEAH, YOU AND ME.

AND ELLEN AND ASH.

HEY, YOU. *NANCY* RIGHT?

YOU'RE ONE OF THE **SICK SISTERS.**

SAYS WHO?

HEH. NOBODY HERE IS OUT TO GET YOU.

I WAS HOPING YOU WERE STILL SELLING?

QUIET THE FUCK DOWN.

REALLY DEPENDS ON WHAT YOU'RE AFTER. I MEAN I GOT SMOKES IF THAT'S YOUR THING BUT THAT'S IT.

SMOKES IS FINE. I JUST NEED TO GET MY EDGE OFF, YOU KNOW?

MIDTERMS.

RIGHT. MEET AFTER SCHOOL AT **THIS LOCATION.** OKAY? ALONE.

ALONE.

OOOOH HOW VERY **SPY VS. SPY.** MAYBE I SHOULD COME AS BACKUP.

AGAINST **THAT** WASTER? PLEASE.

23

BUT THAT'S *FIVE KIDS* NOW. THIS IS GETTING OUT OF *HAND,* SARGE.

IT'S JUST RUNAWAYS, BEN. THAT'S ALL IT IS. AND WE CAN'T INVESTIGATE *EVERY SINGLE RUNAWAY.*

BUT--

LISTEN. THIS TOWN IS FALLING APART. OF COURSE KIDS ARE GONNA BOLT. 90% OF THE TIME THEY'RE BACK HOME IN A MONTH. WE DON'T HAVE THE RESOURCES TO CHASE THEM ALL!

HOW THE HELL DO WE KNOW IF THEY'RE RUNAWAYS WHEN WE HAVEN'T EVEN *LOOKED?*

THIS IS *FIRST CLASS* DERELICTION OF--

LISTEN, BEN. YOU NEED TO DROP THIS BEFORE YOU GET A REPUTATION. AND REPUTATIONS HAVE *CONSEQUENCES.*

YOU WOULDN'T. SIR, I'VE BEEN ON THE FORCE FOR A *DECADE.*

OH, YOU THINK I WOULDN'T? THIS IS A MILLION TIMES BIGGER THAN YOU, YOU LITTLE PIECE OF SHIT.

THERE ISN'T *ANYTHING* I WOULDN'T DO.

WHERE DO YOU THINK YOU'RE GOING?!

¡VEN *PARA ACÁ!* THIS CONVERSATION IS *NOT* OVER!

LOOK WHO FINALLY SHOWED UP!

HOW EMBARRASSED ARE YOU THAT YOU GOT CAUGHT SELLING **SARATOGAS?**

GIRL, WE HAVE **BIGGER SHIT** TO WORRY ABOUT.

I BARELY EVEN KNOW WHERE TO START.

THE BEGINNING IS THE STANDARD PLACE.

ALRIGHT. OKAY. SO. THE DISAPPEARANCES? THE POLICE...

...THE POLICE AREN'T EVEN INVESTIGATING. I THOUGHT IT WAS THAT DUDE'S BAD TRIP, BUT SHIT. I HEARD IT MYSELF.

OKAAAAY...?

I THINK SOMETHING'S GOING ON. AND IT'S TARGETING HIGH SCHOOLERS.

AND THAT MEANS WE'RE **ALL** IN DANGER.

I THINK IT'S UP TO US TO STOP THIS.

CHAPTER 2

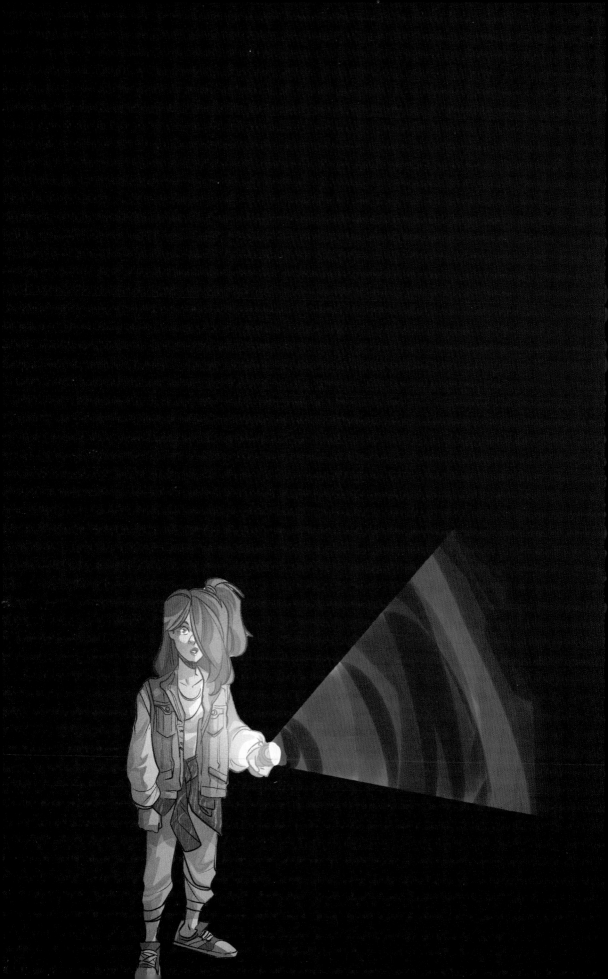

Tucker, Ohio.
1983

SO? ANYTHING WEIRD? UNEXPECTED? *SINISTER?*

NO.

SIR, DO YOU KNOW WHY I PULLED YOU OVER?

CAR 22, WE HAVE REPORTS OF *DOMESTIC DISTURBANCE* ON GINGER STREET.

NANCY, SERIOUSLY, IF THIS CAR BACKS UP EVEN A COUPLE OF *FEET*--

SHHHH!

WE'RE GOING TO *FIND SOMETHING* AND WE'RE GOING TO *BREAK THIS THING WIDE OPEN.*

=SIGH=
FANTÁSTICO,
MOM.

TAP

TAP

DAMN THIS HAD **BETTER** BE RONNIE, OR--

SHIT!

HI! NANCY!

WHAT THE HELL ARE YOU DOING?

I DIDN'T WANT TO BOTHER YOUR FOLKS!

WELL, THEY AREN'T HOME, SO COME ON UP.

ASHLEY, WHAT...

...JESUS, OKAY.

SO.

SOOOOOOOOO. I'VE BEEN THINKING A LOT ABOUT WHAT YOU SAID LAST NIGHT. ABOUT THE POLICE AND EVERYTHING? ABOUT THE **CONSPIRACY**.

I NEVER SAID IT WAS A--

AND I WANTED TO TELL YOU THAT I AM IN.

LIKE, IF THE **POLICE** ARE ALL UNDER THE CONTROL OF SPACE MONSTERS ABDUCTING CHILDREN FOR EVIL EXPERIMENTS, I FIGURE **SOMEONE** SHOULD BE LOOKING INTO IT.

WHO BETTER THAN THE **SICK SISTERS?**

THE NEXT DAY.

WELL, I DIDN'T *FIND* ANYTHING, IF THAT'S WHAT YOU'RE ASKING.

OBVIOUSLY THAT IS *NOT* WHAT I WAS ASKING. I DON'T UNDERSTAND WHY YOU'RE WASTING YOUR TIME WITH THIS. WE HAVE *RECORDS*, NANCY.

WE SHOULD BE *AVOIDING* THE POLICE.

I DUNNO. I MEAN, IT SOUNDS *IMPORTANT.*

DON'T EVEN BOTHER, ASHLEY.

AND YOU'RE NOT EVEN DOING A GOOD *JOB* OF THIS! I'VE READ ENOUGH NANCY DREW TO KNOW THAT JUST... *FOLLOWING PEOPLE AROUND* ISN'T GONNA GET YOU ANYWHERE!

YOU HAVE TO TAKE ACTUAL RISKS, YOU STUPID *PANSY.* NOT TAIL THE FUZZ WITH A BLINKING NEON GODDAMN SIGN OVER YOUR HEAD.

YEAH, I *GUESS* THAT MAKES SENSE.

I MEAN, IF THE POLICE DIDN'T WANT ANYONE TO THINK ANYTHING WAS WRONG, THEY'D ACT NORMAL. GOOD STRATEGY.

SHE'S RIGHT! IF SOMETHING WAS WRONG, NOTHING WOULD *SEEM* WRONG!

FUUCK.

WHAT ARE YOU **DOING** HERE?

WELL IF IT AIN'T THE HARDY GIRL HERSELF.

I'D CALL YOU **NANCY DREW** BUT YOUR NAME IS ALREADY NANCY SO IT'D LOSE A LOT OF ITS PUNCH.

I WANTED TO MAKE SURE YOU DINGUSES DIDN'T **FUCK ANYTHING UP.**

IF YOU GUYS GOT PICKED UP OR WHATEVER, WHO THE HELL WOULD KNOCK OVER MAILBOXES WITH ME? CHELSEA HOWE? **AS IF.**

I'M TOUCHED.

LOOK. LET'S JUST GET THE HELL OUT OF HERE BEFORE SOMETHING GOES **WRONG** AND COUNT IT AS A WASH.

I DON'T KNOW. I THINK THIS THING JUST GOT BIGGER. I MEAN, **LOOK** AT THIS PLACE.

WHY'D THEY... **FLEE** LIKE THIS? IT'S **WEIRD.**

WOOoOOooO

SHIT.

47

OKAY.

LET'S GO.

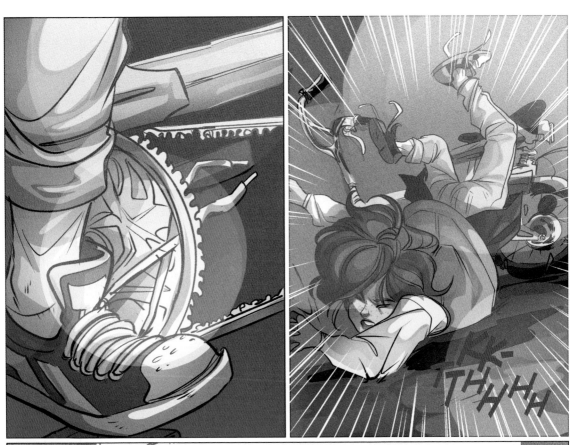

ASH!

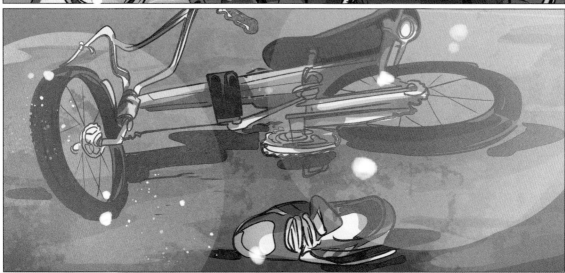

CHAPTER 3

"...AND FIRED."

HOLY *SHIT!*

BRRRNG
BRRRNG

HOTCHKISS RESIDENCE, VERONICA SPEAKING.

HEY, RONNIE.

NANCE! SOMETHING GOING ON? YOU KNOW MY FOLKS GIVE ME SHIT IF I GET CALLS AFTER 9:30.

YEAH, I KNOW. I'M SORRY. BUT IT'S ABOUT ASHLEY.

DID THEY FIND HER? IS SHE OKAY? DID SOMEONE--

RONNIE. CALM DOWN. THEY DIDN'T FIND HER.

NOBODY IS PICKING UP AT HER PLACE.

WHY THE HELL DO **I** GOTTA MAKE THE CALL?

I DON'T SEE HOW THAT OBLIGATES ME TO MAKE THE ACTUAL PHONE CALL.

YOU PICKED UP THE PHONE!

IT'S AN IMPLIED ASSUMPTION OF RESPONSIBILITY! IT'S LIKE CALLING SHOTGUN!

I *LIKE* SHOTGUN! I *HATE* CALLING STRANGERS AT TEN IN THE MORNING!

LOOK. I'LL COVER THE LONG-DISTANCE CHARGES IF YOU DO THE TALKING.

DEAL?

GOD. *FINE.*

KLINK

DOOT DOOT DOOT DOOT DOOT DOOT DOOT DOOT DOOT DOOT

BRRRING

MAYBE SHE WON'T PICK UP.

SHUT UP.

HELLO?

UHHH... UHHH...

HELLO?

HI. SORRY. IS THIS CORINNA POMEROY?

UM, YES, THIS IS SHE.

HI, SO. MY NAME IS VERONICA HOTCHKISS AND MY FRIEND WHO WAS BLANKING INTO THE PHONE IS NANCY SALAZAR. WE'RE **BIG FANS** OF MORTAL DIVIDE AND WE WERE WONDERING IF WE COULD ASK YOU SOME QUESTIONS ABOUT IT?

FOR SCHOOL.

I MEAN, USUALLY PEOPLE JUST SEND FAN MAIL BUT--

IT'S KINDA AN EMERGENCY.

YOU HAVE EMERGENCY QUESTIONS ABOUT A SCI-FI NOVEL? LISTEN, I DON'T REALLY TAKE **PHONE CALLS** FROM FANS--

IS IT TRUE? DID IT HAPPEN? **WILL** IT HAPPEN? IS IT HAPPENING **NOW?**

UH, I MEAN, IT'S **FICTIONAL--**

YEAH, BUT IS IT? BECAUSE THERE'S SOME WEIRD STUFF HAPPENING IN OUR TOWN AND IT FEELS A LOT LIKE MORTAL DIVIDE. UNEXPLAINED DISAPPEARANCES. POLICE ACTING WEIRD. A BIG-ASS MYSTERIOUS FACTORY THAT JUST OPENED UP.

IT'S THE **SAME,** ISN'T IT? THEY TOOK OUR **FRIEND,** MS. POMEROY.

HELLO?

SHIT, I THINK SHE HUNG UP--

I HAVE NO RELATIONSHIP WITH MARATHON TECHNOLOGIES. BUT IF WHAT YOU'RE SAYING IS TRUE...

AND SO.

DING DONG

1610

1610

"IT WAS THE BOHBECK'S ALL OVER AGAIN."

DO YOU KNOW WHAT HAPPENED TO THE FAMILY THAT LIVED HERE?

OH, UH, THAT... THAT PLACE HAS BEEN EMPTY FOR *YEARS*, I THINK.

I GOT THIS ADDRESS FROM THE SCHOOL. A FRIEND OF MINE IS SUPPOSED TO LIVE HERE.

PLEASE DON'T ASK ME ANY MORE QUESTIONS.

I JUST *GOT* THIS JOB.

WHAT?!

I CAN'T SHOW YOU THAT FILE. WE CAN ONLY RELEASE INFORMATION RELATING TO A CASE TO SOMEONE PARTY TO IT, OR A DECEDENT'S NEXT OF KIN.

WHAT THE *FUCK* IS A DECEDENT?

A DEAD PERSON.

WELL, I *AM* THE FAMILY OF THE DECEDENT!

SO I TRUST YOU'LL BE RELEASING THE D'FIORE FILE.

LOOK. IF YOU AREN'T YOUR FRIEND'S LEGAL GUARDIAN, I CAN'T HELP YOU. SO UNLESS YOU CAN SHOW ME A COURT ORDER, I'M GONNA HAVE TO ASK YOU TO LEAVE.

NANCE-- WHAT ARE YOU DOING?

GETTING PROOF WE'RE NOT CRAZY.

THAT'S... WILDLY ILLEGAL.

YOU WANNA TALK TO ME ABOUT ILLEGAL? YOU'RE THE ONE WHO GOT ME SELLING WEED WHEN I WAS THIRTEEN.

WHATEVER THE HELL THAT THING WAS TOOK ASHLEY AND NOBODY IS LOOKING INTO IT BUT US. THEY'RE IN ON IT, WHATEVER THE HELL "IT" IS.

I'M NOT GONNA SIT HERE AND WAIT FOR THE PROBLEM TO SOLVE ITSELF. ASHLEY WAS OUR FRIEND AND SHE'S PROBABLY DEAD AND NOBODY CARES BUT US.

SO I WANT TO MAKE THEM CARE.

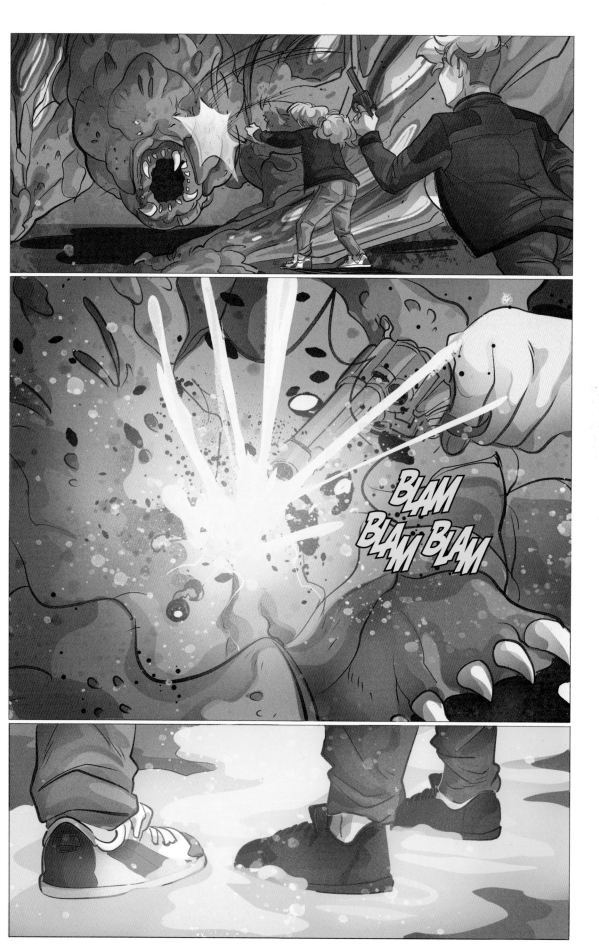

CHAPTER 4

"ASHLEY WAS RIGHT ABOUT *EVERYTHING.*"

WHAT DO YOU MEAN "EVERYTHING"?

I'VE GOT IT ALL SORTED OUT. IT'S REALLY THE ONLY POSSIBILITY.

THE POLICE ARE CONTROLLED BY *TOWN HALL*, WHICH IS CONTROLLED BY *MARATHON TECHNOLOGIES*, WHICH IS A BIG SCARY SECRET FACTORY *CONTROLLED BY SPACE ALIENS IN ORDER TO CONQUER THE EARTH*, JUST LIKE IN MORTAL DIVIDE.

EVERYTHING.

REPTILIAN ROCKET PEOPLE.

EVERYTHING THAT *MATTERED*, ANYWAY.

THE MONSTER WE KILLED IS GONE, BUT THERE'S A TRAIL OF BLOOD--LITERALLY A TRAIL OF BLOOD-- LEADING RIGHT BACK TO THE FACTORY. MUST HAVE LEAKED FROM WHATEVER VAN THEY TOOK IT IN.

SO IT *IS* A CONSPIRACY.

YEAH. A CONSPIRACY WE'RE ALL PAYING FOR.

THIS DOESN'T MAKE ANY SENSE. WHY WOULD THEY OPEN A FACTORY JUST TO KILL EVERYONE?

I DON'T KNOW. MAYBE THEY'RE ALIENS. MAYBE IT'S NOT A FACTORY. MAYBE THEY EAT HUMANS. OR THEY'RE ENSLAVING PEOPLE AND SENDING THEM TO THEIR HOME PLANET.

HELL, THEY COULD BE **SPACE ZOOLOGISTS** AND THIS IS A CATCH-AND-RELEASE PROGRAM.

WHAT IF ALL THIS IS AN ACCIDENT? MAYBE SOMETHING WENT WRONG AND THEY COULDN'T CONTAIN IT.

MAKES AS MUCH SENSE AS ANYTHING ELSE.

WELL, IT CERTAINLY MAKES **MORE** SENSE THAN SPACE ALIEN SLAVERS FROM BEYOND THE MOON.

BUT WHATEVER IS HAPPENING, COPS ARE SITTING ON IT.

WORSE.

THE COPS WERE KEEPING AN EYE ON THAT LOCATION. THEY'RE CLEARLY WORKING WITH MARATHON.

WELL THAT SUCKS.

IF **THEY** WON'T DO ANYTHING, **WE'LL** HAVE TO.

LIKE WHAT? THE THREE OF US STORM A FACTORY FULL OF ARMED GUARDS?

WELL, WE ALREADY KNOW THAT THESE THINGS CAN BE KILLED.

SO LET'S KILL **MORE** OF THEM.

WE GOT **LUCKY**, NANCY. THAT'S ALL. WE DON'T NEED TO BE HUNTING GIANT BAT MONSTERS.

SOUNDS LIKE A GREAT WAY TO GET KILLED.

NO, I SEE WHERE SHE'S GOING WITH THIS. MAYBE THE THREE OF US CAN'T STORM A HEAVILY GUARDED ALIEN PEOPLE-EATING FACTORY, BUT WE CAN DO OUR BEST TO MAKE WHATEVER IT IS THEY'RE DOING AS INCONVENIENT AS POSSIBLE.

BESIDES, WHAT'S STANDING IN THE WAY OF ONE OF THOSE BAT-THINGS PULLING AN ASHLEY ON US, ANYWAY? I MEAN, IF IT'S LITERALLY **EATING KIDS.**

IF NOTHING ELSE, WE MAKE IT HARDER TO DO THAT.

FINE. LET'S HUNT MONSTERS LIKE SOME PLUCKY-ASS REBEL ALLIANCE. IT'S BETTER THAN JUST WAITING TO DIE, ANYWAY.

BUT BEFORE WE MARCH OFF TO OUR CERTAIN DEATHS, LET ME JUST SAY, LADIES...

...IT'S BEEN AN HONOR SERVING WITH YOU.

UM, OKAY.

WHOA!

I'M NOT GOING TO SIT AROUND WHILE YOU WAIT FOR LIFE TO *FIX ITSELF!* THINGS DON'T GET BETTER ON THEIR OWN, LUIS!

CARLA!

DON'T YOU ACT LIKE I DO NOTHING FOR THIS FAMILY! I HAVE GIVEN--

OH? WHAT DO YOU DO EXACTLY? DOES MOPING FOR A LIVING PAY WELL?

IT'S NOT MY FAULT THE GM PLANT SHUT DOWN! YOU THINK THERE'S A LOT OF JOBS FOR *WELDERS* IN THIS CITY?

THERE ARE *OTHER THINGS* YOU COULD DO! YOU'RE SMART! YOU USED TO BE SO *AMBITIOUS!*

YOU WANT ME TO WORK AS A *GROCERY CLERK* FOR MINIMUM WAGE? I'VE WORKED TOO HARD TO BUILD THIS LIFE AND I'M NOT GOING BACKWARDS!

IF MARATHON EVER HIRED *LOCALLY* INSTEAD OF FLYING IN THEIR OWN PEOPLE, MAYBE THERE'D BE OPTIONS.

BUT THEY'VE SHUT THE ENTIRE TOWN OUT! REMEMBER HOW THEY WERE GONNA SAVE THE TOWN? REMEMBER ALL THOSE *JOBS* THEY PROMISED?

WHUNK

NOTHING'S YOUR FAULT, IS IT?

BETWEEN YOUR WHINING AND THAT *LUNATIC* IN OFFICE WAGGING HIS NUCLEAR FINGER AT ANYTHING THAT MOVES, I FEEL LIKE I CAN'T STAND UP STRAIGHT.

I'M *SCARED*, LUIS. I'M SCARED FOR YOU, I'M SCARED FOR NANCY, I'M SCARED FOR EVERYONE.

I CAN'T DO ANYTHING ABOUT THE WORLD. BUT I CAN DO SOMETHING ABOUT MY LIFE AND MY DAUGHTER'S.

THANKS FOR STANDING BY ME.

THIS WASN'T YOU.

IT'S NEVER ABOUT YOU.

WHAT THE HELL AM I DOING, RONNIE?

GONNA GET MYSELF *KILLED*.

THE IMPORTANT THING IS THAT IT WORKS. IN FACT, WE'RE PLANNING ON BEGINNING **FULL OPERATIONS** TONIGHT.

TONIGHT?

YOU DON'T HAVE TO GO THROUGH ALL THAT ON MY ACCOUNT.

YOU MEAN YOU DIDN'T **KNOW?**

I ASSUMED THAT'S WHAT HAD BROUGHT YOU OUT HERE.

NO, NOTHING OF THE SORT. I JUST GOT A PHONE CALL THAT MADE ME THINK OF YOU.

SOMETHING ABOUT MONSTERS, AND DISAPPEARANCES. IT ALL FELT A LITTLE...

...FAMILIAR.

HOLY TOLEDO THIS FOG. CAN'T SEE *SHIT* ANY-MORE.

WHERE THE HELL EVEN *AM* I?

I REMEMBER MAKING A LEFT ON KENNEDY, AND ANOTHER ON IROQUOIS...

KSH

WOOOSH

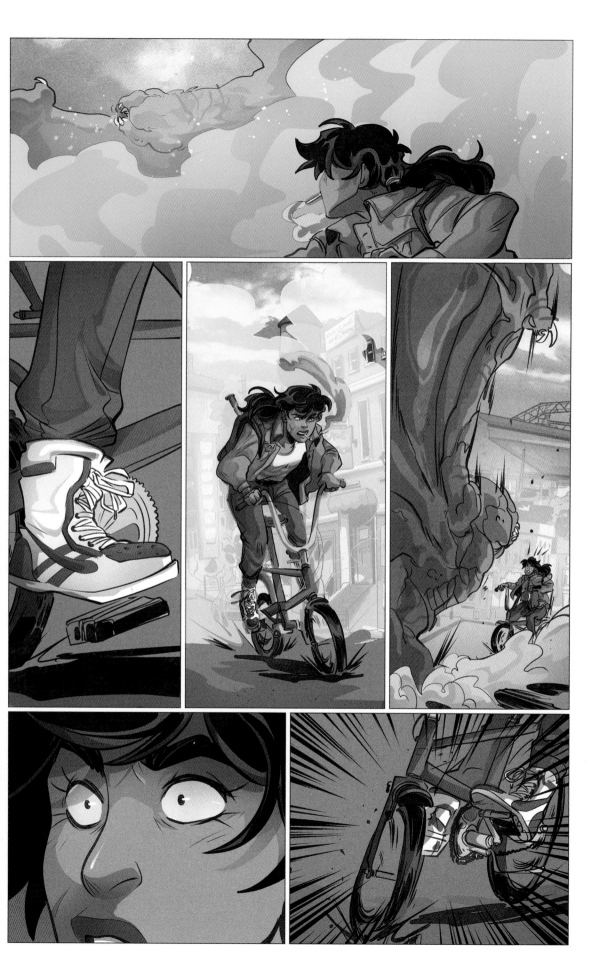

RUMMMA
RUMMMA
RUMMMA
RUMMA

--WHAT--

CHAPTER
5

Tucker, Ohio.
1983

IT'S GONNA BE OKAY, ELLEN.

OUR TOWN IS LITERALLY BEING DESTROYED BY *GODZILLA!*

YEAH. WHICH MEANS WE NEED TO STAY CALM OR WE'LL JUST MAKE THINGS *WORSE.*

GUYS--

HOW COULD THIS GET WORSE?

I DON'T THINK *EITHER* OF US WANTS AN ANSWER TO THAT QUESTION.

GUYS--

THERE'S A...

I SEE IT, RONNIE.

I THINK IT FOLLOWED ME.

ALRIGHT, LADIES. KEEP CALM. STAY FOCUSED.

WE'VE DONE THIS BEFORE.

RONNIE!

WHUNK

ALRIGHT, HOLD IT.

WHERE THE **HELL** DO YOU THINK YOU GIRLS ARE GOING? EVERYONE HAS BEEN ORDERED TO **EVACUATE.**

MY DAD'S STILL IN THERE. I HAVE TO GO GET HIM BEFORE THAT **THING** KILLS HIM.

WE CAN'T LET YOU HEAD INTO THAT PART OF TOWN. IT'S GONNA BE A WAR ZONE.

JUST **THROW 'EM IN THE BACK** AND LET'S GET THE HELL OUT OF HERE WHILE WE CAN.

YOU CAN'T DO THAT!

GET AWAY FROM ME!

WHOA!

I--I THINK YOU NEED TO PUT THAT THING AWAY.

LEAVE. US. ALONE.

I'M NOT GOING TO LEAVE MY DAD TO DIE LIKE AN ANIMAL.

SO PLEASE GET OUT OF MY WAY.

LET 'EM GO, BRADY.

IT DOESN'T MATTER. JUST LET 'EM GO.

WHAT?!

WHAT THE HELL WAS THAT?

WE'RE ALL GONNA DIE ANYWAY, BRADY.

WE'RE ALL GONNA DIE ANYWAY.

NANCE!

WE HAVE TO KEEP **MOVING!**

THAT THING IS FASTER THAN WE ARE, AND HALF THE ROADS ARE GONNA BE IMPASSIBLE BY NOW.

WE HAVE TO GET TO **COVER** BEFORE THE AIR FORCE CARPET-BOMBS OHIO INTO OBLIVION.

SOMETHING BUILT TO WITHSTAND **ANYTHING?**

ASHLEY'S DAD'S **BOMB SHELTER.**

D FIORE

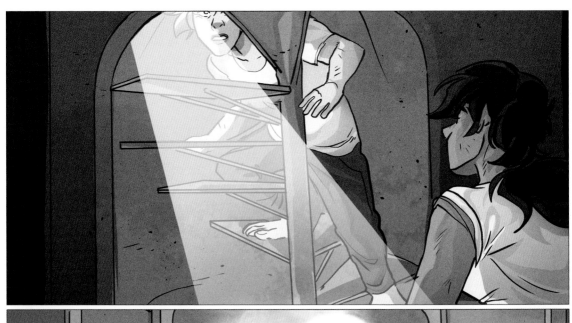

HEY, SARGE!

THERE'S SURVIVORS!

END.

ISSUE #1 ALTERNATE COVER
BY ELIZABETH BEALS

Original Character Designs

NANCY

VERONICA

ELLEN

ASHLEY

NANCY

① ② ③

ASHLEY

① ② ③

ELLEN

① ② ③

VERONICA

① ② ③

ISSUE #2

ISSUE #3

ABOUT THE CREATORS

MAGDALENE VISAGGIO

is the Eisner and GLAAD Media Award-nominated writer behind *Kim & Kim*, *Eternity Girl*, *Dazzler: X Song*, *Transformers vs Visionaries*, and *Morning in America*. A lifelong comics reader, she studied English at Virginia Commonwealth University and did graduate work in Ethics & Moral Theology at Seton Hall before dropping out to focus on writing comics where people hit each other with guitars. When not writing, she's probably passed out on her couch at three in the morning with a cat on top of her while Netflix asks if she wants to continue watching *Star Trek: The Next Generation*. She lives in Manhattan.

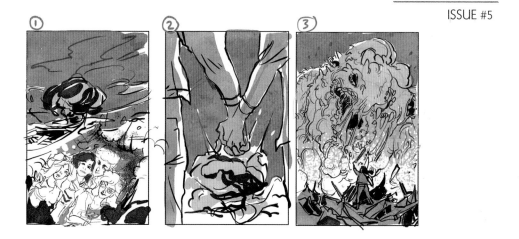

CLAUDIA AGUIRRE
is a queer comic book artist and writer. She's a GLAAD Award Nominee, Will Eisner Award nominee, and a co-founder of Boudika Comics, where she self-publishes comics. She has worked for Black Mask, Oni Press, Legendary, Limerence Press, and Boom! Studios.

ZAKK SAAM
is a comic book letterer from Detroit, Michigan known for his work on *Kim & Kim* and *Star Trek/Green Lantern*. When not lettering, Zakk can be most often found on the ice rink with the Motor City Mayhem, an adult hockey club he co-founded in 2009, or throwing dice at a D&D table. He now lives in mid-Michigan with his girlfriend and their four dogs.

OPEN EARTH
BY SARAH MIRK, EVA CABRERA, AND CLAUDIA AGUIRRE

Rigo, a young woman living aboard a space station just after the collapse of Earth, explores her own desires by developing openly polyamorous relationships with her friends and crewmates.

RICK AND MORTY™ PRESENTS, VOL. 1
BY MAGDALENE VISAGGIO, DANIEL MALLORY ORTBERG, J. TORRES, DELILAH DAWSON, CJ CANNON, AND MORE

Learn the secret stories and hidden pasts of your favorite *Rick and Morty*™ characters in this comic collection, featuring fan-favorite characters and storylines.

THE BUNKER, VOL. 1
BY JOSHUA HALE FIALKOV AND JOE INFURNARI

Five friends find mysterious letters addressed to each of them... from their future selves. Told they will destroy the world, can they avoid making the wrong choices? Or will an even darker fate engulf the world?

KIM REAPER, VOL. 1: GRIM BEGINNINGS
BY SARAH GRALEY

Becka has a big crush on Kim, but she doesn't know that Kim works part-time as a grim reaper! Can they figure out their budding romance while avoiding the consequences of the underworld?